Sally Dog Little

Text by Bill Richardson + Illustrations by Céline Malépart

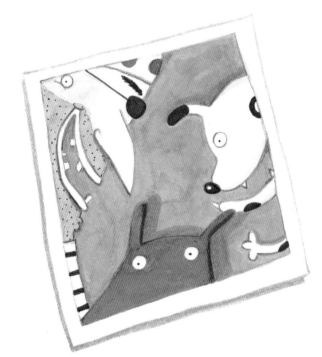

ANNICK PRESS

TORONTO + NEW YORK + VANCOUVER

When the Little family got a dog, they named her Sally Dog Little. Sally Dog Little is what they always called her. They never called her Sally, for short. The Littles were a formal family. Formal families are not fond of "for short." On the day that Sally Dog Little came to stay, each of the Littles took her aside and told her what they wanted her to be.

"I want you to be a proper dog and bark only when burglars come," said Papa. He was very, very formal indeed.

"I want you to be a proper dog and walk with me morning, afternoon, and evening," said Mama. She was very formal and also very fit.

"I want you to be a proper dog and to sleep on my bed at night and to cuddle up close," said Twinkle Little, who was still too young to be truly formal, but for whom her parents had great hopes.

Sally Dog Little commenced her working life.
She was glad to sleep on the bed.
"What a good dog," said Twinkle Little,
each and every morning.

She enjoyed the walking.
"What a good dog," said Mama Little,
as they huffed and puffed along.
And since burglars never came calling, there
was never any need for Sally Dog Little to bark.
"What a good dog," said Papa Little, who liked
his dogs quiet and his house burglar free.
Everything was fine and everyone was happy.

But then, one day, a ghost pirate and his ghost dog walked right through the wall of the house and into the Littles' formal living room.

"Arf, arf, arf," said Sally Dog Little, for she knew that pirates were also likely to be burglars.

"Arf, arf, arf," she said, and then for good measure she added,

"**Bow wow wow!**"

"Burglars!" cried Papa Little. He ran into the room carrying a poker with which to poke the burglar.

"Burglars!" cried Mama Little. She ran into the room carrying a skillet with which to crack the burglar on the noggin.

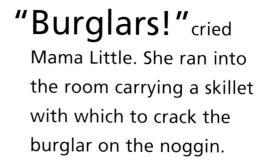

"Burglars!" cried Twinkle Little. She ran into the room carrying a camera with which to take the burglars' picture, so that she would have something for Show and Tell at school.

But when they reached the living room, what did they see? Why, nothing at all. That was because the pirate and his dog were ghosts, and the Littles were far too formal to see something that was made only out of air. All they saw was Sally Dog Little, and all they heard was her barking.

"Arf, arf, arf! Bow wow wow!" she said, and for good measure she added, **"Woof, woof, woof."**

"Be quiet, Sally Dog Little," said Papa. "Proper dogs never bark for no good reason. If this happens again, you will have to go."

"Be quiet, Sally Dog Little," said Mama. "Proper dogs never bark for no good reason. If this happens again, I shall have to go walking by myself."

"Say cheese, Sally Dog Little," said Twinkle, who didn't see when the ghost pirate and his dog also smiled for the camera.

"Who are you?" asked Sally Dog Little, when they had all gone away.

"I'm Swiggity Jim the Pirate, and this is my dog, Needles."

"Are you burglars?" asked Sally Dog Little.

"Have been," said Swiggity Jim, "back in the good old days, a long time ago. Now we're but a couple of ghosts, on our way to the place where ghosts go. The trouble is, we can't get there till we lay our mitts on one priceless piece of treasure."

"Why are you here?"
"See, we left treasure in so many places, we can't remember where we stashed the one thing we need. So, we've been visiting all the places we buried our booty. A cool oasis in sunny Sudan. A pretty pagoda in distant Japan. A cave above Rio where few dare to wander. And under the oak you see growing out yonder."

Swiggity Jim pointed to the big old shade tree in the Littles' formal garden.

"There's buried treasure in my backyard?"

"Yep. Can you help us dig it up?"

Sally Dog Little thought and thought. If Swiggity Jim and Needles didn't find their treasure, they might stay and stay, and she might be tempted to bark and bark. She knew what that would mean.

"All right," said Sally Dog Little. "But not until after dark."
"Dandy," said Swiggity Jim.
   And they stretched out on the formal sofa where dogs
   were forbidden and pirates would never be encouraged.

That night, when all the Littles were deep in their formal
dreams, Sally Dog Little met Swiggity Jim and Needles outside.
"There," pointed Swiggity Jim, and Sally Dog Little began to dig.
She dug and she dug for a very long time.
"Are you sure?" she asked.
"Aye aye," said Swiggity Jim. "You're getting close."

So she dug and she dug and she dug some more until she finally hit metal.

"Har, har," said Swiggity Jim, shining his lantern into the hole. "Paydirt!"
Needles and Swiggity Jim danced a hornpipe while Sally Dog Little hauled up a chest.

"Har, har," said Swiggity Jim again, when the chest was opened. "Goodness," said Sally, as she gazed upon gold, diamonds, doubloons, rubies, a wooden leg, and one very large bone. Tacked onto the inside lid of the treasure trunk was a tattered old map. Swiggity Jim pointed to it and cried, "There! That's what we've been looking for."

The ghost pirate and his dog studied the map, muttering to each other, and turning their heads this way and that.
"Got it, Needles?" asked Swiggity Jim, and Needles nodded yes.
"Then it's time we were going."

"But what about the treasure?" asked Sally Dog Little. "Aren't you going to take it with you?"

"Nope," answered Swiggity Jim. "Where we're bound, we won't need treasure. Help yourself to anything you can use and bury the rest for someone else to find."

And they disappeared, just like that, without even saying
thank you or good luck.
Sally Dog Little thought and thought. She thought for a long,
long time before she made up her mind.

Morning came. Twinkle Little woke. Sally Dog Little
was beside her, just as she always was.
"Why, Sally Dog Little," said Twinkle.
"Where did you get that bone?"
The sun shone down on the Littles' house and yard.
There was not a trace of anything like a hole
under the oak.

To Bill on the one hand and to Mac on the other.

© 2002 (text) by Bill Richardson
© 2002 (illustrations) by Céline Malépart

Annick Press Ltd.

We acknowledge the support of the Canada Council for the Arts, the Ontario Arts Council, and the Government of Canada through the Book Publishing Industry Development Program (BPIDP) for our publishing activities.

Copy editing by Elizabeth McLean
Design by Irvin Cheung / iCheung Design
The art in this book was rendered in watercolor
The text was typeset in Frutiger

Cataloguing in Publication Data

Richardson, Bill, 1955-
        Sally Dog Little

ISBN 1-55037-759-0

        I. Malépart, Céline II. Title.

PS8585.I186S22 2002   jC813'.54   C2002-900486-1
PZ7.R39428Sa 2002

Manufactured in China

Published in the U.S.A. by
Annick Press (U.S.) Ltd.

Distributed in Canada by
Firefly Books Ltd.
3680 Victoria Park Avenue
Willowdale, ON
M2H 3K1

Distributed in the U.S.A. by
Firefly Books (U.S.) Inc.
P.O. Box 1338
Ellicott Station
Buffalo, NY 14205

Visit our website at **www.annickpress.com**